Walt Disney's CLASSIC
Sleeping Beauty

Illustrated by Ron Dias

A GOLDEN BOOK · NEW YORK
Western Publishing Company, Inc., Racine, Wisconsin 53404

In a faraway land, long ago, King Stefan and his fair queen wished for a child. At last a daughter was born to them, and they named her Aurora.

To honor the baby princess, the king held a great feast. Nobles and peasants, knights and their ladies—everyone flocked joyfully to the castle.

King Stefan welcomed his good friend King Hubert to the feast. King Hubert had brought his young son, Phillip, with him. The kings agreed that someday Phillip and Aurora would be married.

Among the guests were three good fairies, Flora, Fauna, and Merryweather. Each of these magic beings wished to bless the infant with a gift.

Waving her wand, Flora chanted, "My gift shall be the gift of Beauty."

"And mine," said Fauna, "shall be the gift of Song."

Merryweather's turn was next. But before she could speak, the castle doors flew open.

Lightning flashed. Thunder rumbled. A tiny flame appeared and grew quickly into the form of the evil witch Maleficent. Her pet raven was perched on her shoulder.

Maleficent was furious, for she hadn't been invited to the feast. Now she took revenge.

"I, too, have a gift for the newborn babe," she sneered. "She shall indeed grow in grace and beauty. But before the sun sets on her sixteenth birthday, she shall prick her finger on the spindle of a spinning wheel...and *die*!"

With a cruel laugh, the witch vanished. Everyone in the room was grief-stricken.

But Merryweather still had a gift to give, and she tried to undo Maleficent's curse. She said to the infant:
"If through this witch's trick
A spindle should your finger prick,
Not in death, but just in sleep
The fateful prophecy you'll keep,
And from this slumber you shall wake
When true love's kiss the spell shall break."

King Stefan ordered that every spinning wheel in the land be burned. But he still feared the witch's curse, so the good fairies hatched a plan. They would take Aurora to live with them, deep in the woods. There she would be safe from Maleficent until her sixteenth birthday.

The king and queen agreed. They watched with heavy hearts as the fairies hurried from the castle, carrying the baby princess.

To guard their secret, the fairies disguised themselves as peasant women and called Aurora Briar Rose. The years passed quietly, and Briar Rose grew into a beautiful young woman.

At last the princess reached her sixteenth birthday. Planning a surprise, the fairies sent her out to pick berries. Fauna baked a cake for her, while the others sewed her gown.

In a mossy glen, Briar Rose danced and sang with her friends, the birds and animals. She told them of her beautiful dream about meeting a tall, handsome stranger and falling in love.

A handsome young man came riding by. When he heard Briar Rose singing, he jumped from his horse and hid in the bushes to watch her. Then he reached out to take her hand.

Briar Rose was startled. "I didn't mean to frighten you," the young man said, smiling. "But I feel as if we've met before."

Briar Rose felt very happy as she and her admirer gazed into each other's eyes. The young man didn't know she was Princess Aurora. And she didn't know he was Prince Phillip, to whom she had been promised in marriage many years before.

Back at the cottage, the fairies gave Briar Rose her birthday surprises. Then Briar Rose told them that she had fallen in love.

"Impossible!" they cried. They told her the truth at last—that she was a royal princess, promised at birth to be married to a prince. Now it was time for her to return home.

So poor Aurora was led away, pining for her handsome stranger.

Maleficent's raven, perched on the chimney of the cottage, had heard everything. It flew off to warn Maleficent that the princess was finally returning to her rightful home.

Maleficent sped to the castle. There, using her evil powers, she lured Aurora to a high tower. In the tiny room, a spinning wheel suddenly appeared.

"Touch the spindle!" hissed Maleficent. "Touch it, I say!"

The three good fairies rushed to the rescue, but they were too late.
Aurora had touched the sharp spindle and instantly fallen into a deep
sleep. Maleficent's curse—softened by Merryweather—had come true.
Now, with a harsh laugh, the witch vanished.

The fairies wept bitterly. "Poor King Stefan and the queen," said Fauna.

"They'll be heartbroken when they find out," said Merryweather.

"They're not going to," said Flora. "We'll put them *all* to sleep until the princess awakens." So the three fairies flew back and forth, casting a dreamlike spell over everyone in the castle.

Meanwhile, the witch had captured Phillip and chained him in her dungeon. "To think," she gloated, "that in the topmost tower of King Stefan's castle is the sleeping Princess Aurora, who, as Briar Rose, won your heart yesterday. She can be awakened only by her true love's kiss— but you'll never find her!" Maleficent laughed evilly as she went out.

Soon after she had gone, the fairies suddenly appeared in the dungeon. They magically freed Prince Phillip from his chains.

Arming Phillip with the Shield of Virtue and the Sword of Truth, the fairies sent him racing to the castle, to awaken the princess.

The witch, seeing Phillip escaping, furiously tried to stop him. She hurled heavy boulders at him, but the brave prince rode on.

When Phillip reached Aurora's castle, Maleficent caused a forest of thorns to grow up all around it. Phillip angrily hacked the thorns aside with his sword.

In a rage, the witch soared to the top of the highest tower. There she changed into a monstrous dragon. "Now you shall deal with *me,* O Prince," she shrieked, "and all the Powers of *Evil*!"

Maleficent breathed huge waves of flame. Phillip ducked behind his strong shield.

Thunder cracked! Flames roared around him! The prince fought bravely. Guided by the good fairies, he flung his magic sword straight as an arrow. It buried itself deep in the dragon's evil heart, and the beast fell to its death. Maleficent was no more.

Phillip raced to the tower where his love lay sleeping. Gently he kissed her. Aurora's eyes slowly opened. She was awake!

Then everyone else awoke, smiling. The king and queen were overjoyed to see Aurora again. They were delighted to find that their daughter and King Hubert's son were in love. They soon made wedding plans.

The good fairies were blissful, too. It had all ended just the way it should—happily ever after.